Dear Parent:

Congratulations! Your child is taking the first steps on an exciting journey. The destination? Independent reading!

STEP INTO READING® will help your child get there. The program offers five steps to reading success. Each step includes fun stories and colorful art. There are also Step into Reading Sticker Books, Step into Reading Math Readers, Step into Reading Write-In Readers, Step into Reading Phonics Readers, and Step into Reading Phonics First Steps! Boxed Sets—a complete literacy program with something for every child.

Learning to Read, Step by Step!

Ready to Read   Preschool–Kindergarten
• big type and easy words • rhyme and rhythm • picture clues
For children who know the alphabet and are eager to begin reading.

Reading with Help   Preschool–Grade 1
• basic vocabulary • short sentences • simple stories
For children who recognize familiar words and sound out new words with help.

Reading on Your Own   Grades 1–3
• engaging characters • easy-to-follow plots • popular topics
For children who are ready to read on their own.

Reading Paragraphs   Grades 2–3
• challenging vocabulary • short paragraphs • exciting stories
For newly independent readers who read simple sentences with confidence.

Ready for Chapters   Grades 2–4
• chapters • longer paragraphs • full-color art
For children who want to take the plunge into chapter books but still like colorful pictures.

STEP INTO READING® is designed to give every child a successful reading experience. The grade levels are only guides. Children can progress through the steps at their own speed, developing confidence in their reading, no matter what their grade.

Remember, a lifetime love of reading starts with a single step!

To Kelsey, a fairy fan
—T.R.

Visit us on the Web!
www.stepintoreading.com
www.randomhouse.com/kids/disney

Educators and librarians, for a variety of teaching tools, visit us at
www.randomhouse.com/teachers

Library of Congress Cataloging-in-Publication Data
Redbank, Tennant.
The great fairy race / by Tennant Redbank. — 1st ed.
    p. cm. — (Step into reading. Step 3 book)
Summary: In the Great Fairy Race no fairy can use her own wings or legs, and so they compete on various animals and contraptions as each tries to prove she is fastest, but all run into a mess of trouble, except Lily, who creeps along atop a snail.
ISBN 978-0-7364-2524-7 (trade pbk.) — ISBN 978-0-7364-8060-4 (lib. bdg.)
[1. Racing—Fiction. 2. Fairies—Fiction.] I. Title.
PZ7.R24455Gre 2008
[E]—dc22
2007029194

Printed in the United States of America   10 9 8 7 6 5 4 3 2 1   First Edition

The Great Fairy Race

By Tennant Redbank

Illustrated by the Disney Storybook Artists

Random House 🏠 New York

"On your marks!"

Queen Clarion called.

"Get set...."

She raised her hands in the air.

"Go!" Queen Clarion shouted.

A light flashed across the sky.

The Great Fairy Race was on!

The rules of the Great Fairy Race
were simple.

The first one to cross the finish

line was the winner.

But the fairies could not

use their own feet or wings.

No running.

No flying.

Beck rode a squirrel.
Right behind her
was Fawn on a frog.
Rani flew through the air
on Brother Dove's back.

Fira soared
in a balloon.

Silvermist surfed on a wave.

Tinker Bell
rode a machine
she had made
out of pots and pans.

And Lily sat high atop

a giant snail.

"Hurry, Lily," Bess called,

"or you will come in last!"

Lily laughed.

"I don't care," she said.

"I like the view up here."

"Coming through!"

Silvermist yelled.

She sailed past Beck.

Now she was first!

But then Fawn's frog
made a mighty jump.
He hopped
right over Silvermist!

"This fairy race is all mine!"
Fawn crowed.

"Not for long," Rani said.
She passed Fawn
from above.

Lily was far behind the others.

But she didn't mind.

She even stopped

to water a flower

next to the path.

"I'll get there soon enough,"

she said.

The fairies crossed the stream.

They tore through the meadow.

They rounded the Home Tree.

They zoomed past the gardens.

But fairy after fairy
ran into trouble.
Beck's squirrel saw
another squirrel.
He ran off to play.

"Turn around!"

Beck cried in Squirrel.

"We're going the wrong way!"

The squirrel scampered up a tree.

Beck was stuck going with him!

Fawn laughed at Beck.
But then her frog
spotted a fat fly
over the pond.

Splash!

Before she knew it,

Fawn and the frog

were in the pond.

The frog was happy.

Fawn was not.

"See you at the finish line!"

Tink called to Fawn.

A minute later,
the wheels of Tink's machine
got stuck in the mud.
"I'll never win now!"
Tink moaned.

Fira's balloon sprang a leak.

It took Fira ten minutes

to fix the hole.

Poor Bess got lost.

She knew she was somewhere

between the mossy rocks

and the crooked tree.

But where?

She took a map

out of her pocket.

"Which way?"

she asked herself.

Rani saw a pretty waterfall.
She stopped to look at it
and fell behind.

Silvermist was not watching
where she was headed.
She sailed into a spiderweb
and got stuck.

Before long,

Beck and Fawn had their animals

under control.

Tink dug out her machine.

Bess found her way.

Rani and Silvermist

were on track again.

"I see the end!"

Fira yelled.

They raced for the finish line.

They were neck and neck,

and wing to wing.

Who was going to be first?

Who would win

the Great Fairy Race?

The fairies put on

a last burst of speed.

They were almost there. . . .

All of a sudden,

Tink's front wheel

ran over the squirrel's tail!

Tink and Beck

and the squirrel went down.

"Nuts and bolts!"

Tink groaned.

Fawn and her frog

were right behind them.

They could not stop!

Fawn's frog jumped and tripped.

It bumped into

Rani and Brother Dove.

Brother Dove crashed into
Fira's balloon.
The balloon lost air
and headed for the ground.

Bess and Silvermist
went down, too.

Not one of the fairies
made it across the finish line.

But wait!

Slowly, slowly,

Lily and her snail inched forward.

They passed Bess.

"Are you taking a rest, Bess?"

Lily asked.

Lily and her snail

passed Fira.

They passed Rani and Tink

and Beck and Fawn

and Silvermist.

"So who won the race?"

Lily asked.

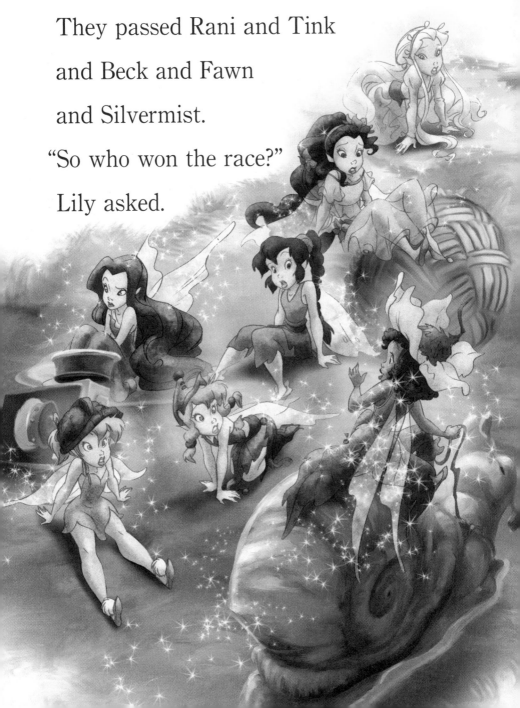

Then Lily and her giant snail
crossed the finish line!

"Lily is the winner!"

Queen Clarion cried.

"I am?" Lily asked.

Lily looked with surprise
at the other fairies.
"I thought the race
was already over,"
she said.

The fairies cheered for Lily.
"Hooray for Lily
and her snail!"
everyone called.

Queen Clarion put a necklace
of flowers around Lily's neck.
She put one around
the snail's neck, too.

"Who knew
a snail would be
the fastest creature
in Pixie Hollow?"
Queen Clarion said.